WOMBAT STEW

Marcia K. Vaughan

Illustrated by
Pamela Lofts

ASHTON SCHOLASTIC
SYDNEY AUCKLAND NEW YORK TORONTO LONDON

For Mum and Dad with love.

Vaughan, Marcia.
    Wombat Stew.

    For children.
    ISBN 0 86896 285 6
    ISBN 0 86896 258 9 (pbk.).

    I. Title.

A823.3

This edition published in 1985 by Ashton Scholastic Pty Limited A.C.N. 000 614 577,
PO Box 579, Gosford 2250. Also in Brisbane, Melbourne, Adelaide, Perth and
Auckland, NZ.

Reprinted in 1986 (twice), 1987 (twice), 1988 (twice), 1989, 1990 (twice), 1991, 1992
(twice), 1993 (twice) and 1994 (twice).

Printed in Hong Kong.

24 23 22 21 20 19 18 17   4 5 6 7 8 / 9

One day, on the banks of a billabong,
a very clever dingo caught a wombat…

and decided to make...

Wombat stew,
Wombat stew,
Gooey, brewy,
Yummy, chewy,
Wombat stew!

Platypus came ambling up the bank.

'Good day, Dingo,' he said,
snapping his bill.
'What is all that water for?'

'I'm brewing up a gooey, chewy stew
with that fat wombat,'
replied Dingo
with a toothy grin.

'If you ask me,' said Platypus,
'the best thing for a gooey stew is mud.
 Big blops of billabong mud.'

'Blops of mud?' Dingo laughed.
'What a good idea.
 Righto, in they go!'

So Platypus scooped up big blops of mud
with his tail
and tipped them into the billycan.

Around the bubbling billy,
Dingo danced and sang...

'Wombat stew,
Wombat stew,
Gooey, brewy,
Yummy, chewy,
Wombat stew!'

Waltzing out
from the shade of the ironbarks
came Emu.
She arched her graceful neck
over the brew.

'Oh ho, Dingo,' she fluttered.
'What have we here?'

'Gooey, chewy wombat stew,'
boasted Dingo.

'If only it were a bit more chewy,'
she sighed. 'But don't worry.
A few feathers will set it right.'

'Feathers?' Dingo smiled.
'That would be chewy!
Righto, in they go!'

So into the gooey brew
    Emu dropped
  her finest feathers.

Around
   and around
the bubbling billy,
Dingo danced and sang...

'Wombat stew,
Wombat stew,
Crunchy, munchy,
For my lunchy,
Wombat stew!'

Old Blue Tongue the Lizard
came sliding off his sun-soaked stone.

'*Sss*illy Dingo,' he hissed.
'There are no flies*ss* in this *sss*tew.
Can't be wombat *sss*tew
without crunchy flies*ss* in it.'
And he stuck out
his bright blue tongue.

'There's a lot to be said for flies,'
agreed Dingo, rubbing his paws together.

'Righto, in they go!'

So Lizard snapped
one hundred flies from the air
with his long tongue
and flipped them into the gooey,
chewy stew.

Around
and around
and around
the bubbling billy,
Dingo danced and sang...

'Wombat stew,
Wombat stew,
Crunchy, munchy,
For my lunchy,
Wombat stew!'

Up through the red dust popped Echidna.

'Wait a bit. Not so fast,' he bristled,
shaking the red dust from his quills.
'Now, I've been listening
to all this advice –
and take it from me,
for a munchy stew
you need slugs and bugs
and creepy crawlies.'

Dingo wagged his tail.
'Why, I should have thought of that.
Righto, in they go!'

So Echidna dug up all sorts of creepy crawlies and dropped them into the gooey, chewy, crunchy stew.

The very clever Dingo stirred and stirred,
all the while singing...

'Wombat stew,
Wombat stew,
Hot and spicy,
Oh so nicey,
Wombat stew!'

Just then the sleepy-eyed Koala
climbed down the scribbly gumtree.

'Look here,' he yawned,
'any bush cook knows
you can't make a spicy stew
without gumnuts.'

'Leave it to a koala to think of gumnuts,'
Dingo laughed and licked his whiskers.

'Righto, in they go!'

And into the gooey, chewy, crunchy,
munchy stew
Koala shook lots and lots of gumnuts.

'Ah ha!' cried Dingo.
'Now my stew is missing only one thing.'

'What's that?' asked the animals.

'That fat wombat!'

'Wait!'

'Stop!'

'Hang on, Dingo!
You can't put that wombat
into the stew yet.'

'Why not?'

'You haven't tasted it.'

'Righto! I'll taste it!'

And that very clever dingo
bent over the billy
and took a great, big slurp of stew.

‘I’m poisoned!’ he howled.
‘You’ve all tricked me!’

And he dashed away
deep into the bush,
never again to sing...

'Wombat stew,
Wombat stew,
Gooey, brewy,
Yummy, chewy,
Wombat stew!'